For Jeff, Shelley, and Harper,
who were there from the start
—T. M.

To my niece, Eleonora
—R. K.

SIMON & SCHUSTER BOOKS FOR YOUNG READERS • An imprint of Simon & Schuster Children's Publishing Division • 1230 Avenue of the Americas, New York, New York 10020 • Text © 2024 by Tim McCanna • Illustration © 2024 by Ramona Kaulitzki • Book design by Chloë Foglia • All rights reserved, including the right of reproduction in whole or in part in any form. • SIMON & SCHUSTER BOOKS FOR YOUNG READERS and related marks are trademarks of Simon & Schuster, LLC. • Simon & Schuster: Celebrating 100 Years of Publishing in 2024 • For information about special discounts for bulk purchases, please contact Simon & Schuster Special Sales at 1-866-506-1949 or business@simonandschuster.com. • The Simon & Schuster Speakers Bureau can bring authors to your live event. For more information or to book an event, contact the Simon & Schuster Speakers Bureau at 1-866-248-3049 or visit our website at www.simonspeakers.com. The text for this book was set in Argone. • The illustrations for this book were rendered digitally. Manufactured in China • 0724 SCP • First Edition
2 4 6 8 10 9 7 5 3 1
Library of Congress Cataloging-in-Publication Data
Names: McCanna, Tim, author. | Kaulitzki, Ramona, illustrator.
Title: Cold / Tim McCanna ; illustrated by Ramona Kaulitzki.
Description: First edition. | New York : Simon & Schuster Books for Young Readers, 2024. |
"A Paula Wiseman Book." | Audience: Ages 4–8. | Audience: Grades 2–3. | Summary: "This lyrical environmental picture book introduces readers to some of the most beautiful and fascinating cold climate creatures and habitats all over the world"— Provided by publisher.
Identifiers: LCCN 2023050789 (print) | LCCN 2023050790 (ebook) | ISBN 9781665940504 (hardcover) | ISBN 9781665940511 (ebook)
Subjects: CYAC: Stories in rhyme. | Animals–Fiction. | Habitat (Ecology)–Fiction. | Cold–Fiction. | LCGFT: Stories in rhyme. | Picture books.
Classification: LCC PZ8.3.M459285 Co 2024 (print) | LCC PZ8.3.M459285 (ebook) | DDC [E]–dc23
LC record available at https://lccn.loc.gov/2023050789
LC ebook record available at https://lccn.loc.gov/2023050790

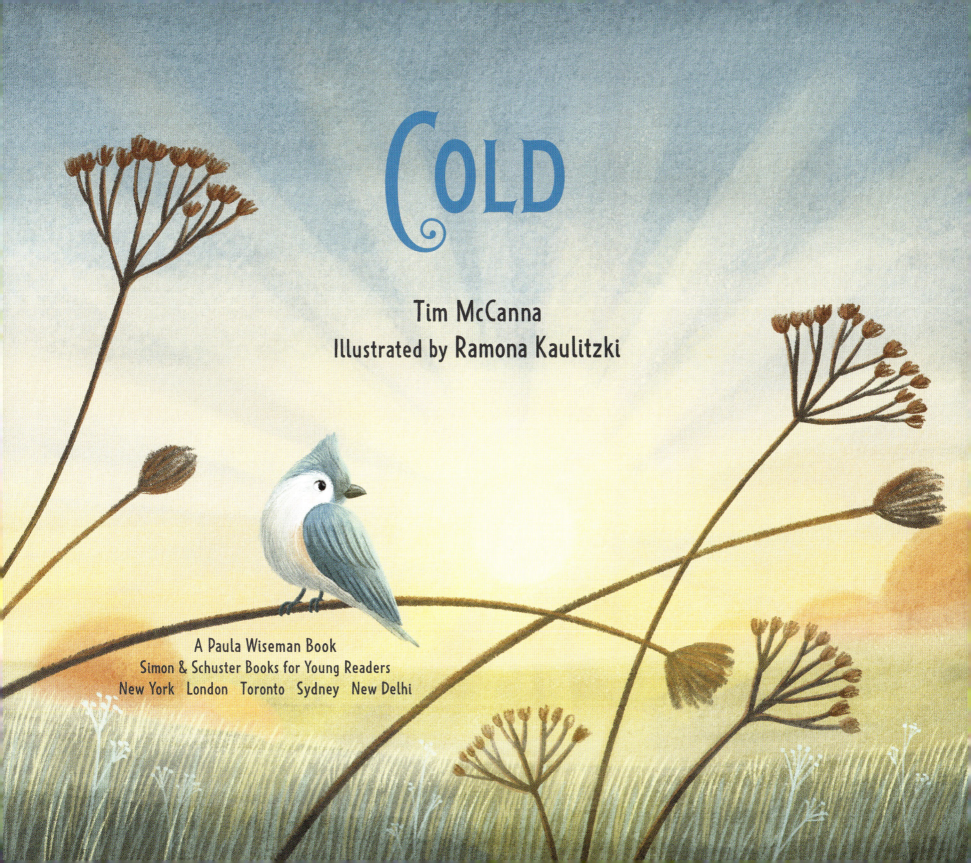

COLD

Tim McCanna

Illustrated by Ramona Kaulitzki

A Paula Wiseman Book
Simon & Schuster Books for Young Readers
New York   London   Toronto   Sydney   New Delhi

Cold is a morning
dappled in dew,
a canvas of sky painted yellow and blue.

Over a mountain
misty and gray,
a hawk braves the chill of a midwinter's day.

Cold is a river
rushing on stone,
the slow, steady beat of its murmuring drone.

Under an ocean
swirling and deep,
a host of inhabitants hover and creep.

Cold is a forest
high on a hill,
the crackle of leaves lying frozen and still.

Chirps in a cavern
far below ground—
a colony flitters and flutters around.

Cold is a meadow
hidden in fog;
a home in the heart of a hollowed-out log.

Towering icebergs
lumber along,
adrift in the waves of a faraway song.

Cold is a desert
shrouded by night;
a hunter goes prowling in shimmering light.

Flurries of snowflakes
ride on a breeze
and dance to the whistle of wind in the trees.

Covered in blankets
of new-fallen snow,
communities forage where little can grow.

Cold is a feeling,
a quiver, a quake
that sinks to the bone till you shiver and shake.

Told in a whisper,
a howl, or a hum—
a promise of marvelous moments to come.

Here in our world
there is much to behold,
where life finds a way when the weather is cold.

What is cold?

Cold is defined as a temperature that is lower than the temperature of the human body. But everyone feels cold differently. What you consider unbearably cold weather might seem comfortable to someone else. A person's healthy internal temperature is 98.6°F (37°C). A cool fall day might be around 60°F (15.5°C). The freezing point when water becomes ice is 32°F (0°C).

What causes cold temperatures?

On maps we divide our planet into northern and southern hemispheres. For each hemisphere, the passing of seasons occurs at different times of the year. Winter, the coldest season, occurs when a hemisphere tilts away from the sun. Wind and moisture in the air can also create a chilling effect. Scientists have found liquid water as cold as -40°F (-40°C). Nights are cold because the heat from the sun is on the other side of the globe. Since caves are underground, they are blocked from the sun and maintain cool temperatures.

Do animals feel cold?

Yes, but not quite like humans do. Animals can sense a range of temperatures. But compared to humans, most warm-blooded animals have a higher tolerance for cold temperatures. Animals are also well adapted to their environments. Their fur, feathers, and thick hides help keep them warm. Some animals hibernate in the winter to conserve body heat and energy, while others eat as much as they can to add fat to their bodies to survive the cold months.

Why is winter necessary?

During cold winter months, snow cover helps regulate the temperature of Earth's surface. When the snow melts, it helps feed rivers and reservoirs. Winter allows plants and trees to go dormant so they can store up energy for new growth in the spring. Winter helps cut back on bugs like mosquitoes, which carry diseases. Seasons are also important for animals. Changes in weather and length of days tell animals when to eat, rest, find a mate, build a nest, or store food. However, seasons are currently being impacted by climate change around the world.

What is climate change?

Climate change refers to planet-wide shifts in temperatures and weather patterns. Some causes of those changes, such as volcanic eruptions, are natural. But since the 1800s, human use of fossil fuels like coal and oil has created gases in the atmosphere that increase Earth's temperature. Winters around the world have grown warmer due to climate change.

How does climate change affect animals?

Wild animals are directly impacted by climate change. Increasingly rising global temperatures cause harsher storms, droughts, heat waves, rising sea levels, and warming oceans that harm animals and destroy their habitats. When glaciers melt, polar bears are forced onto land and lose access to their hunting grounds. As oceans grow warmer, they increase in volume, causing sea levels to rise. During long droughts, farmers lose their crops, while storms and floods can destroy homes and whole communities.

What can *YOU* do to help combat climate change?

Lots of things! Carpool to school to cut back on using gas. Walk or bike when you can. Turn off lights when you leave a room to reduce your energy usage. Take shorter showers to save water. Plant trees that absorb toxic carbon dioxide and release clean oxygen into the atmosphere. Grow a garden to help avoid soil erosion. Shop locally to cut down on transportation pollution. Wear an extra layer during cold weather rather than turning up the heat. Avoid single-use items like plastic water bottles that wind up in landfills. Recycle and reuse containers. You can also support your favorite not-for-profit groups that help protect wildlife, preserve the environment, and combat global climate change.